EL GLOBO GRANDE Y MOJADO

The big wet balloon

SPANISH EDITION

LiNiErs

EL GLOBO GRANDE Y MOJADO

The big wet balloon

A SPANISH EDITION TOON BOOK BY

LINIERS

TOON BOOKS IS AN IMPRINT OF CANDLEWICK PRESS

Dedicado a Matilda y Clementina...mis pequeñas musas

Editorial Director: FRANÇOISE MOULY

Book Design: FRANÇOISE MOULY & RICARDO LINIERS SIRI

Consultant to the Spanish Edition: JOSÉ SANTIAGO

LINIERS' artwork was done in ink and watercolor, and drops of rain.

A TOON Book™ © 2013 Liniers & RAW Junior, LLC, 27 Greene Street, New York, NY 10013. TOON Books® is an imprint of Candlewick Press, 99 Dover Street, Somerville, MA 02144. No part of this book may be used or reproduced in any manner whatsoever without written permission except in the case of brief quotations embodied in critical articles and reviews. TOON Books®, LITTLE LIT® and TOON Into Reading™ are trademarks of RAW Junior, LLC. All rights reserved. Printed in Johor Bahru, Malaysia by Tien Wah Press (Pte.) Ltd.

The Library of Congress has catalogued the hardcover English-language edition as follows:

Liniers, 1973-

The big wet balloon : a TOON book / by Liniers.

pages cm. – (Easy-to-read comics. Level 2)

Summary: "Matilda promises her little sister Clemmie an amazing weekend spent playing outside. But the weather's rainy and Clemmie can't bring her new balloon along. Matilda teaches Clemmie all the delights of a wet Saturday"– Provided by publisher.

ISBN 978-1-935179-32-0 (alk. paper)

1. Graphic novels. [1. Graphic novels. 2. Sisters–Fiction. 3. Rain and rainfall–Fiction. 4. Balloons–Fiction.] I. Title.

PZ7.7.L56Bi 2013   741.5'973–dc23   2012047662   ISBN: 978-1-935179-32-0 (hardcover English edition)

ISBN: 978-1-935179-40-5 (hardcover Spanish edition)   ISBN: 978-1-935179-39-9 (paperback Spanish edition)

13 14 15 16 17 18 TWP 10 9 8 7 6 5 4 3 2 1

WWW.TOON-BOOKS.COM

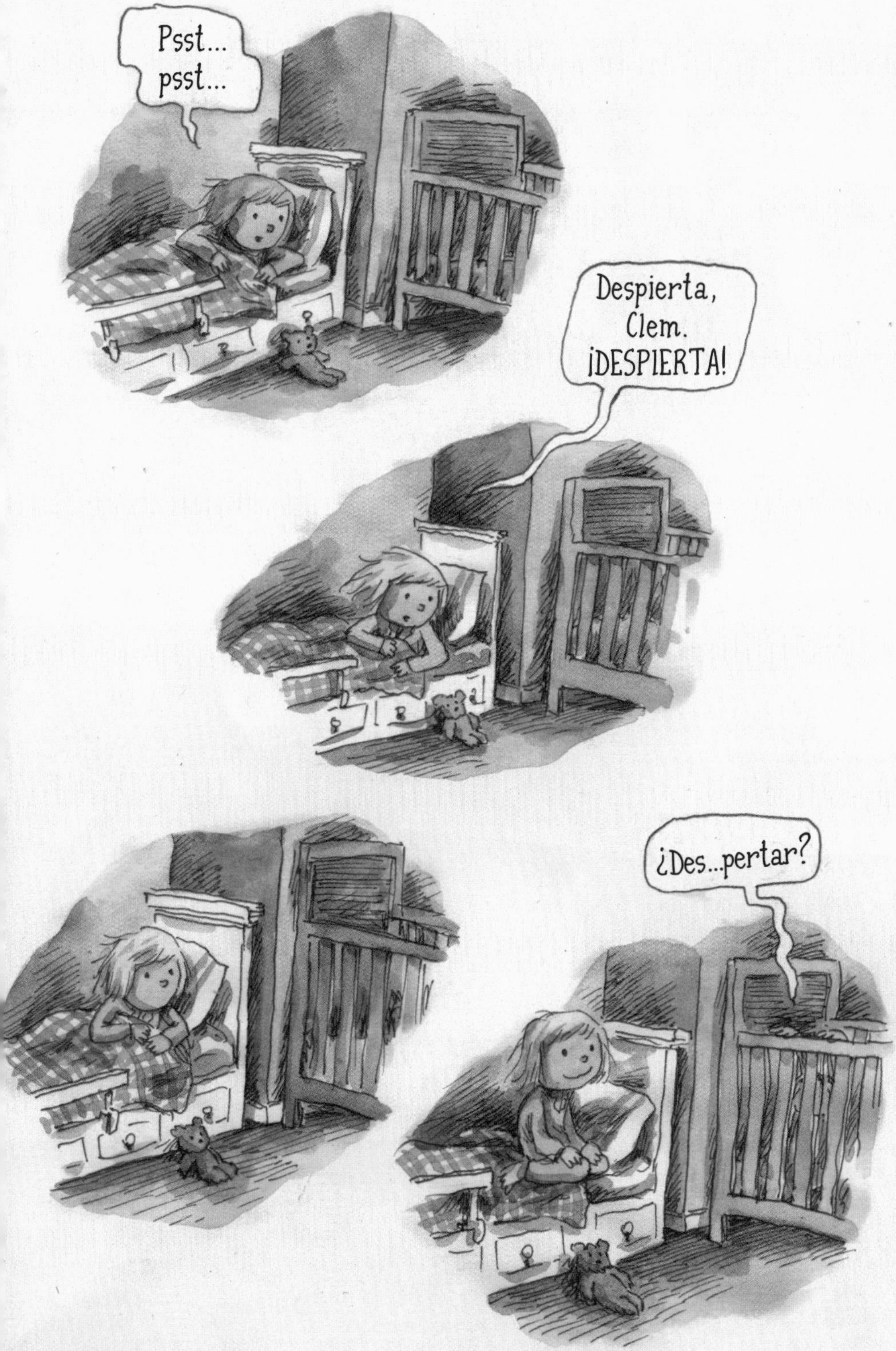
Psst...
psst...
Despierta,
Clem.
¡DESPIERTA!
¿Des...pertar?

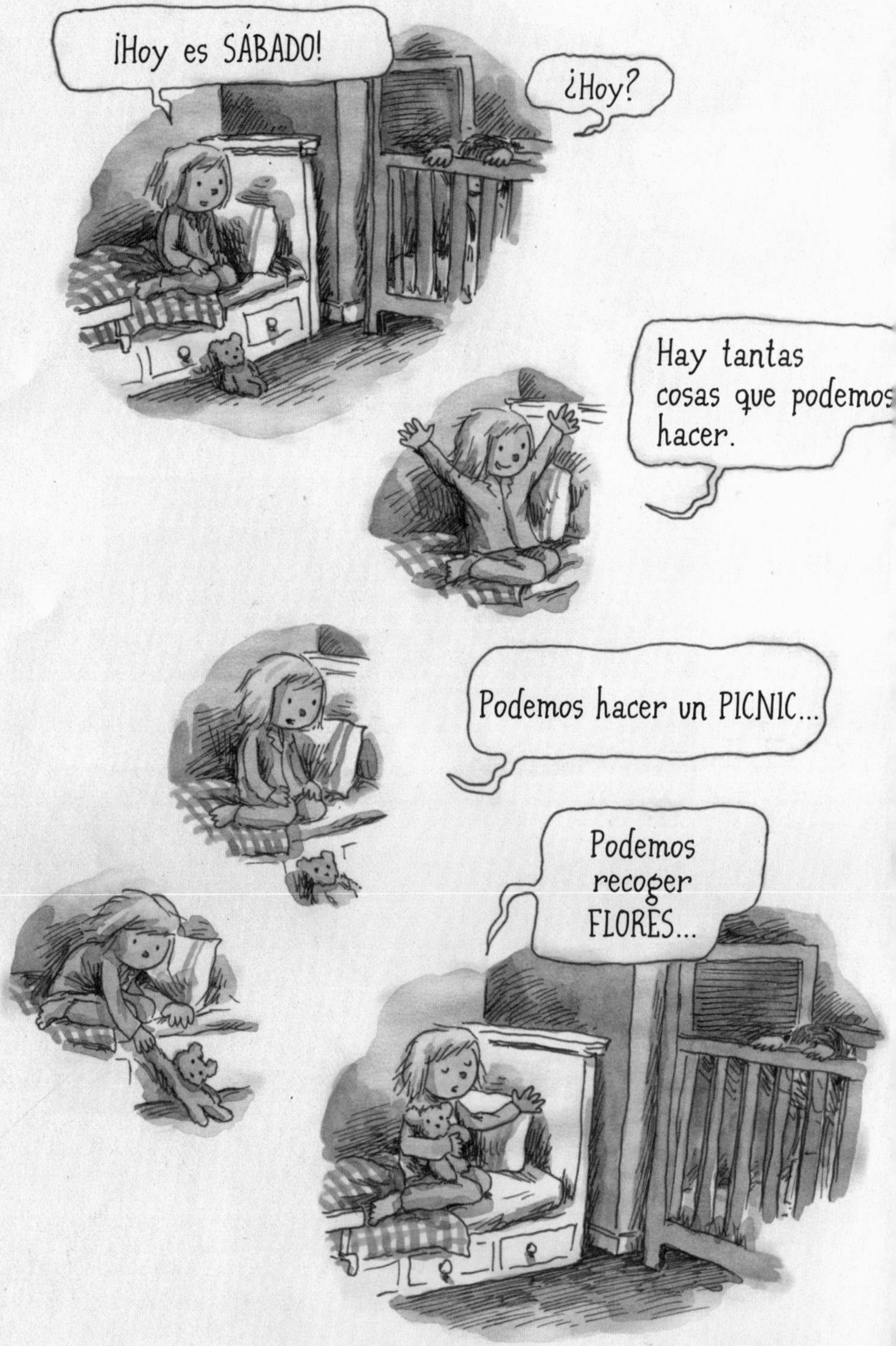
¡Hoy es SÁBADO!
¿Hoy?
Hay tantas cosas que podemos hacer.
Podemos hacer un PICNIC...
Podemos recoger FLORES...

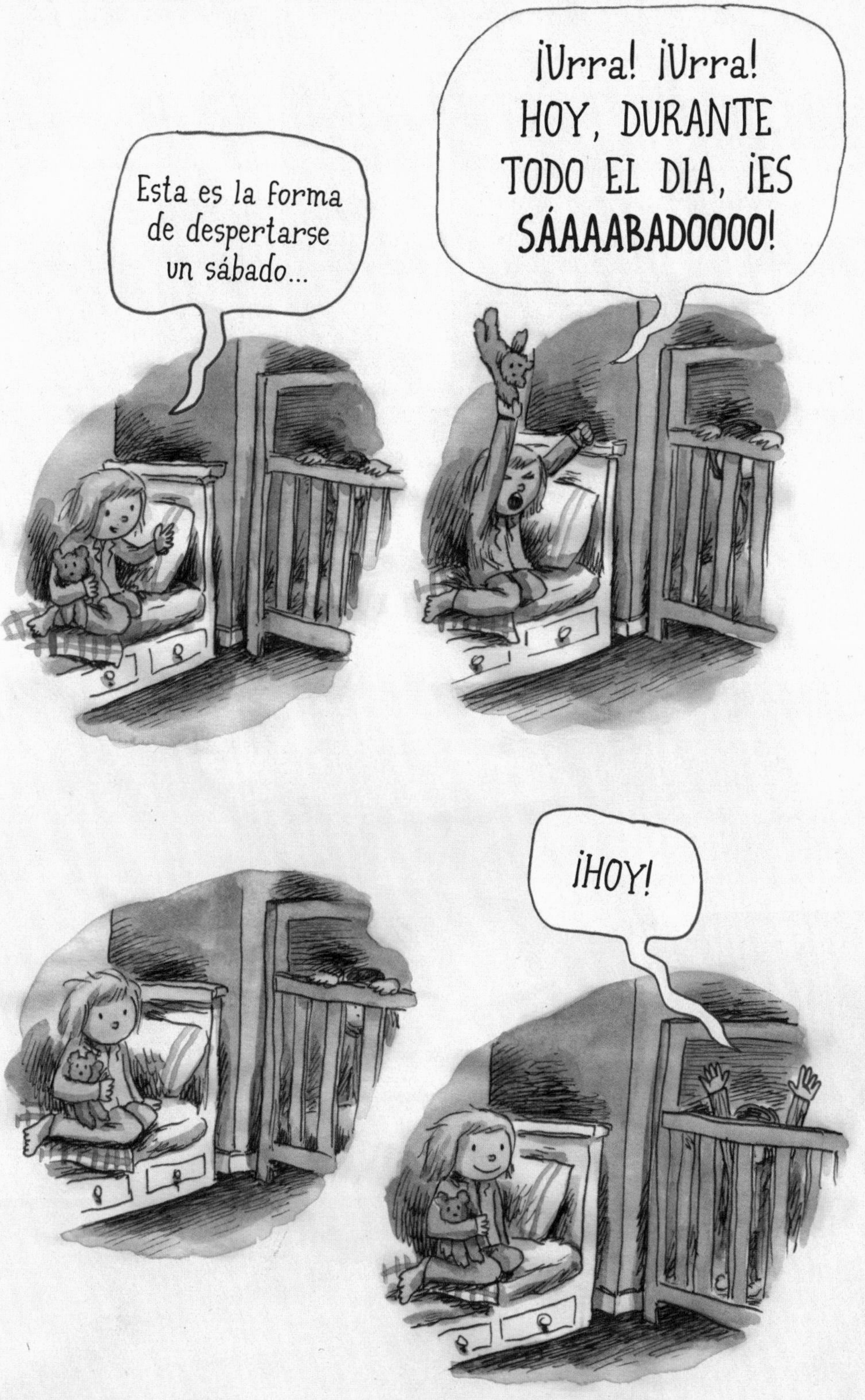
Esta es la forma de despertarse un sábado...
¡Urra! ¡Urra! HOY, DURANTE TODO EL DIA, ¡ES **SÁAAABADOOOO**!
¡HOY!

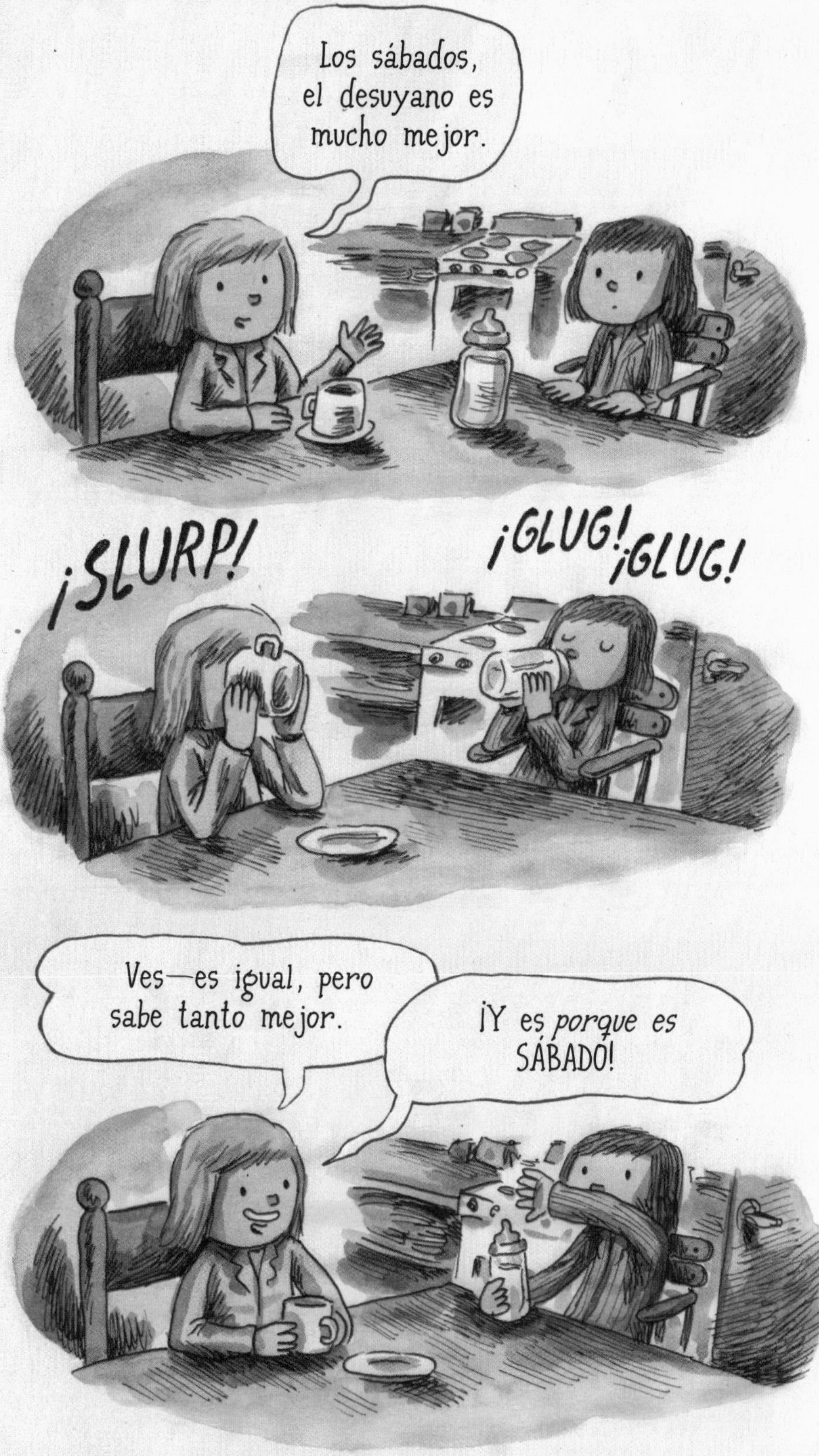
Los sábados, el desuyano es mucho mejor.
¡SLURP!
¡GLUG! ¡GLUG!
Ves—es igual, pero sabe tanto mejor.
¡Y es *porque* es SÁBADO!

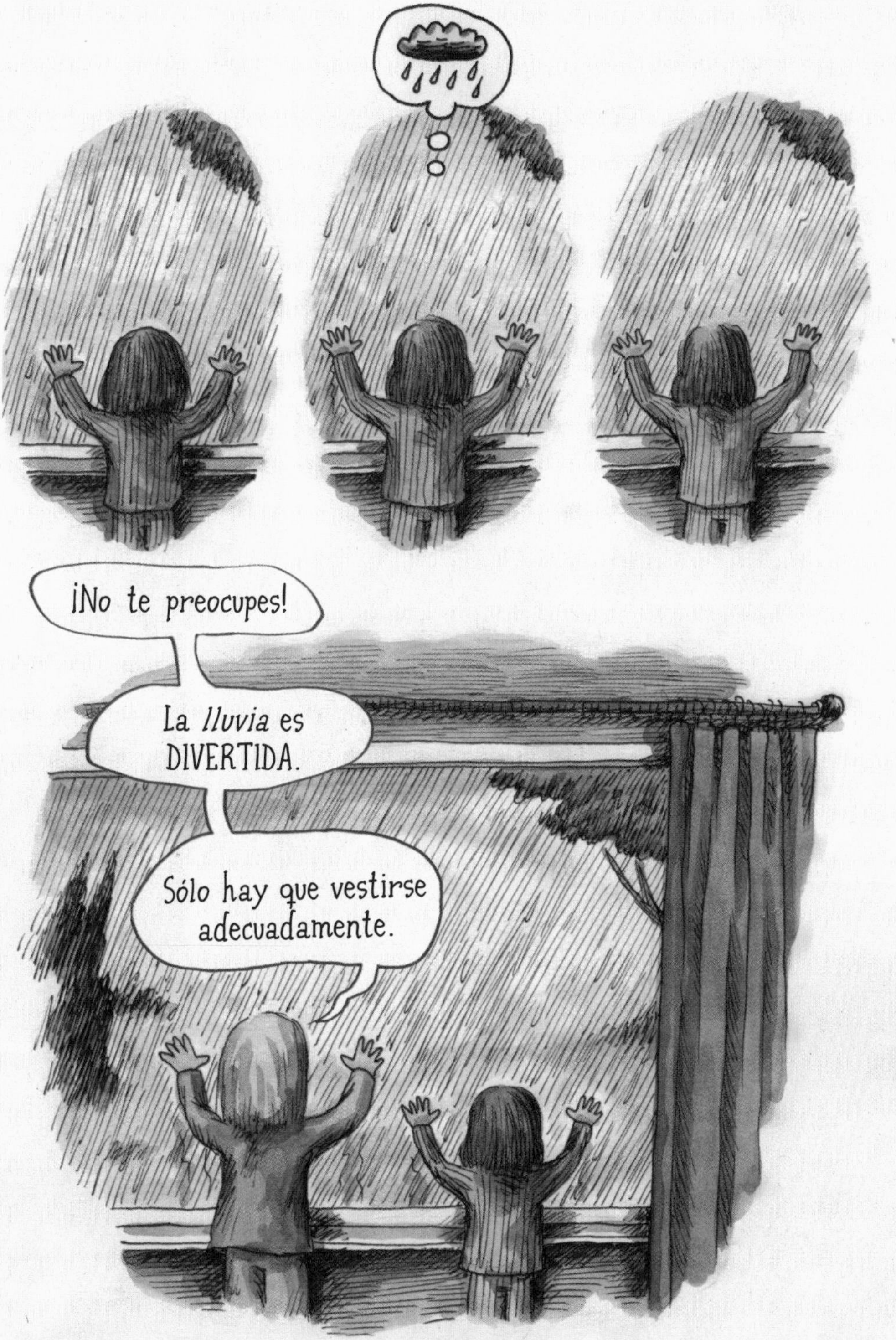
¡No te preocupes!
La *lluvia* es DIVERTIDA.
Sólo hay que vestirse adecuadamente.

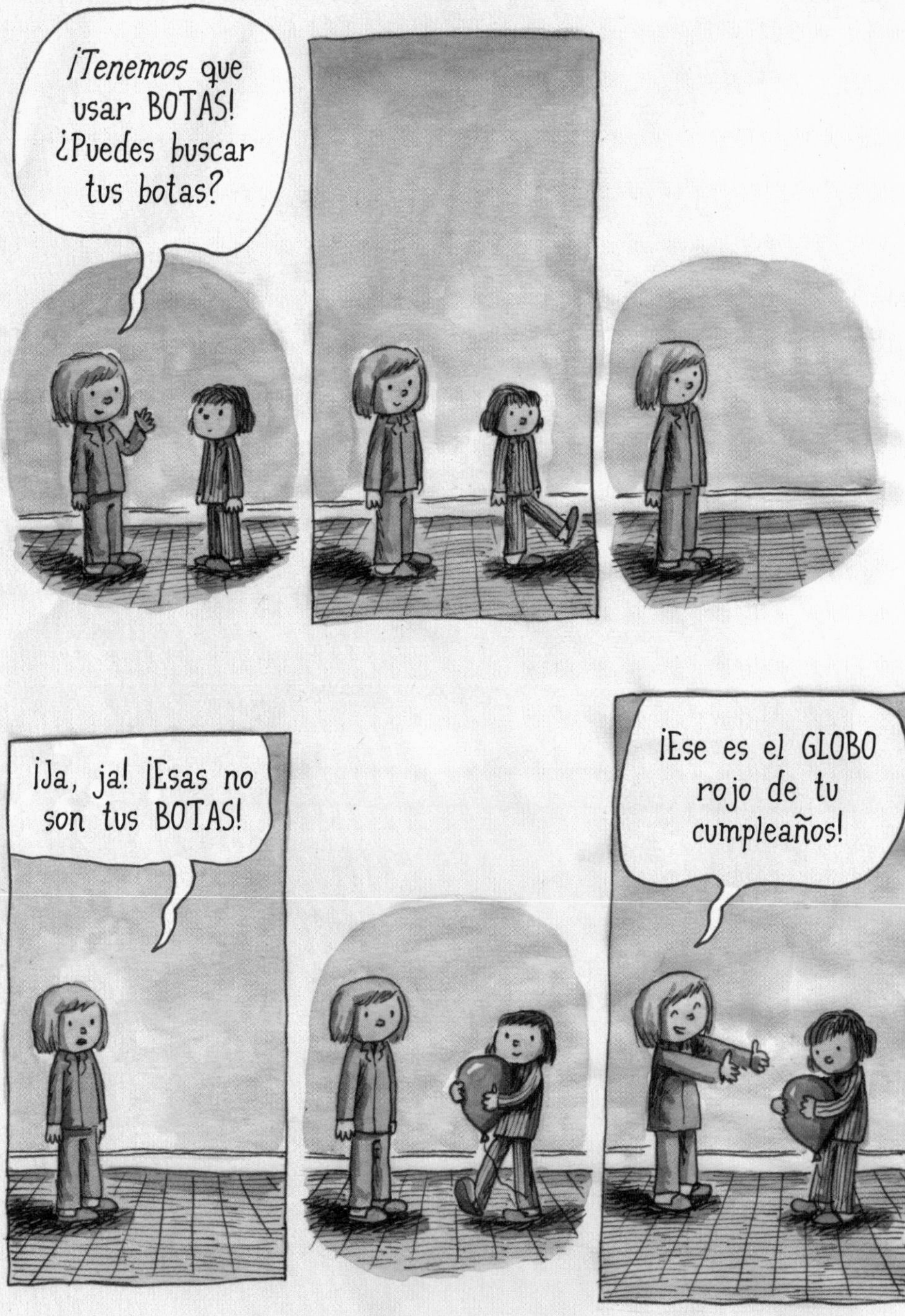
¡Tenemos que usar BOTAS! ¿Puedes buscar tus botas?
¡Ja, ja! ¡Esas no son tus BOTAS!
¡Ese es el GLOBO rojo de tu cumpleaños!

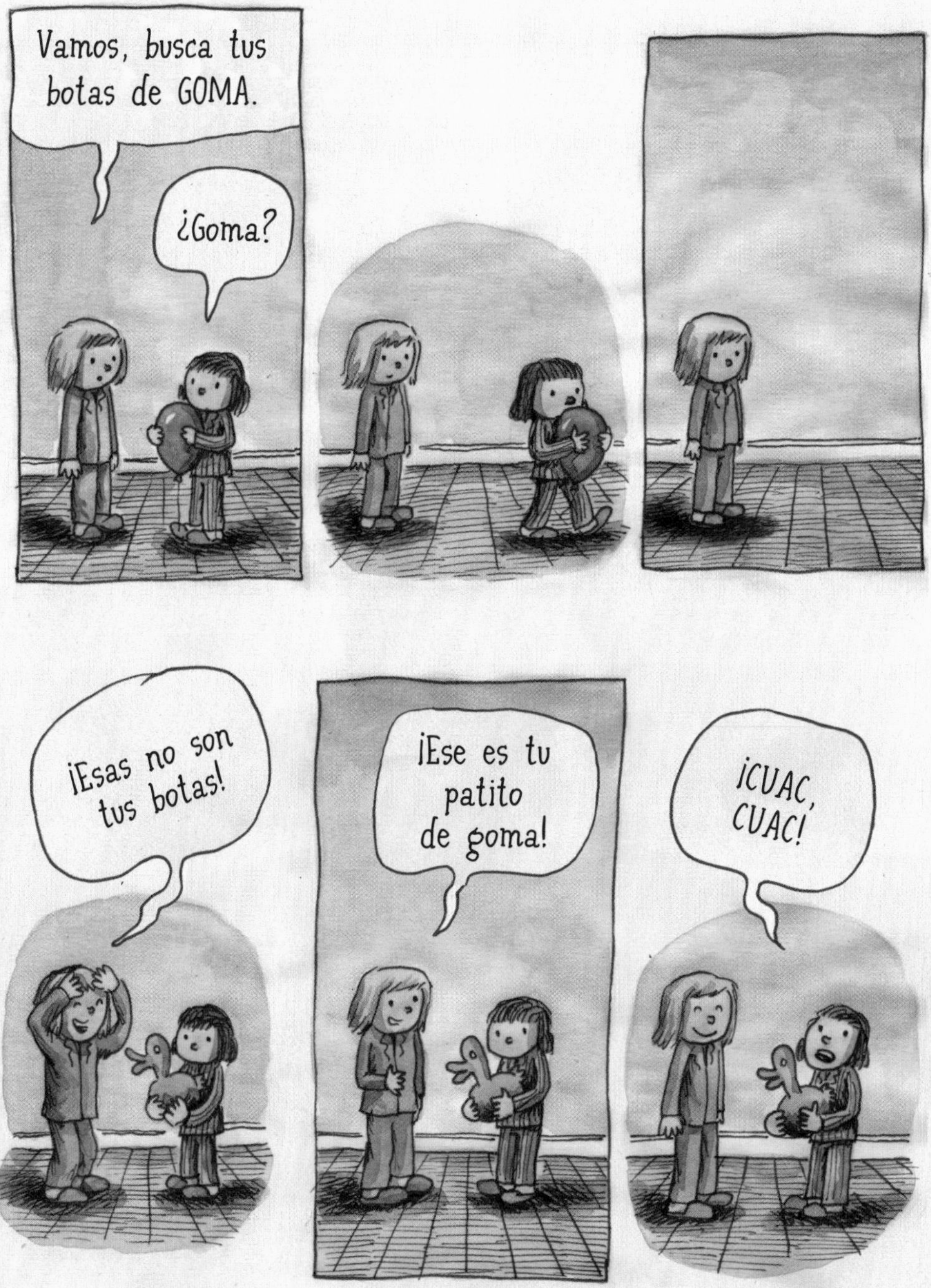

Vamos, busca tus botas de GOMA.
¿Goma?
¡Esas no son tus botas!
¡Ese es tu patito de goma!
¡CUAC, CUAC!

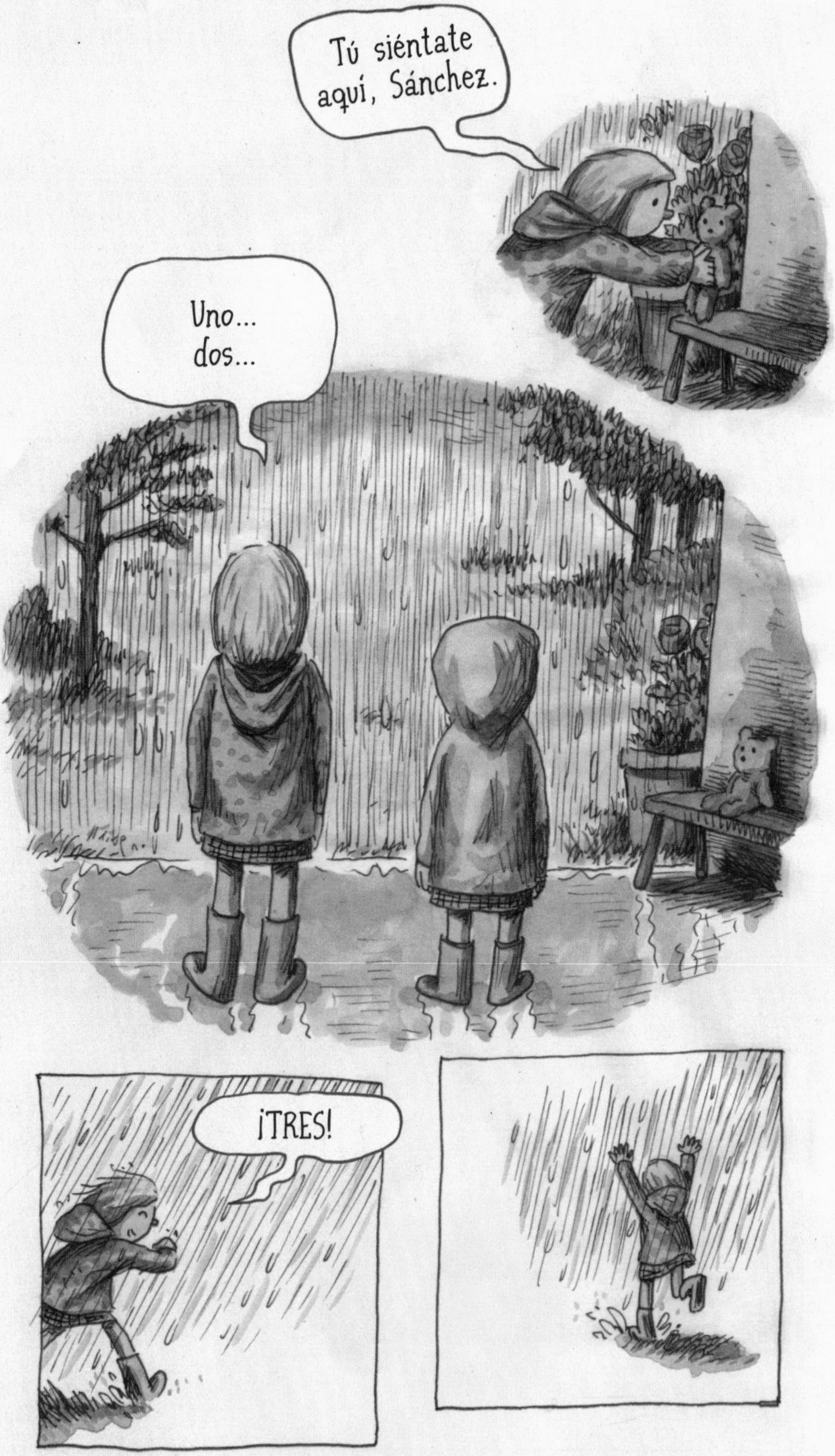
Tú siéntate aquí, Sánchez.
Uno... dos...
¡TRES!

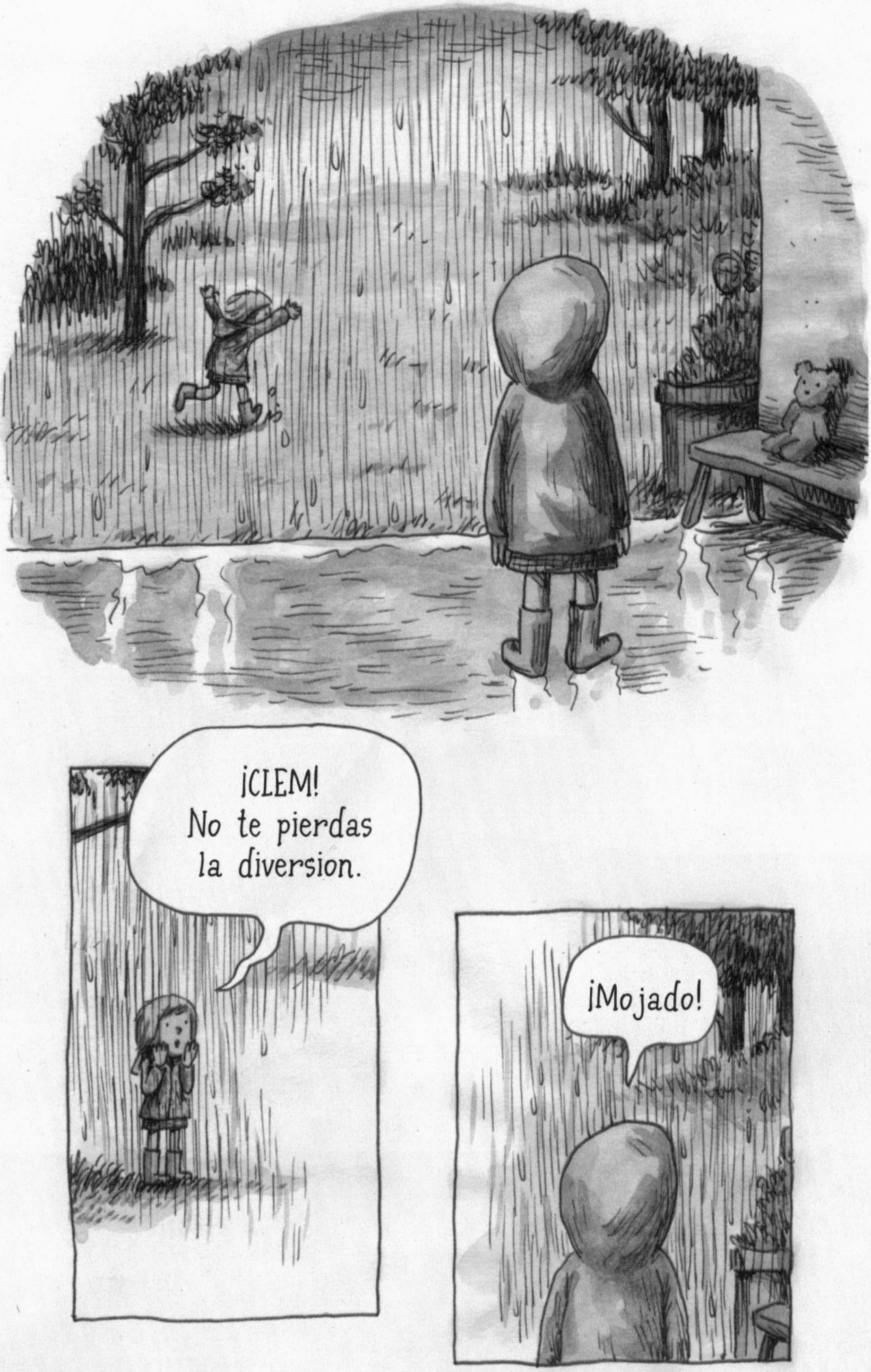
¡CLEM! No te pierdas la diversion.
¡Mojado!

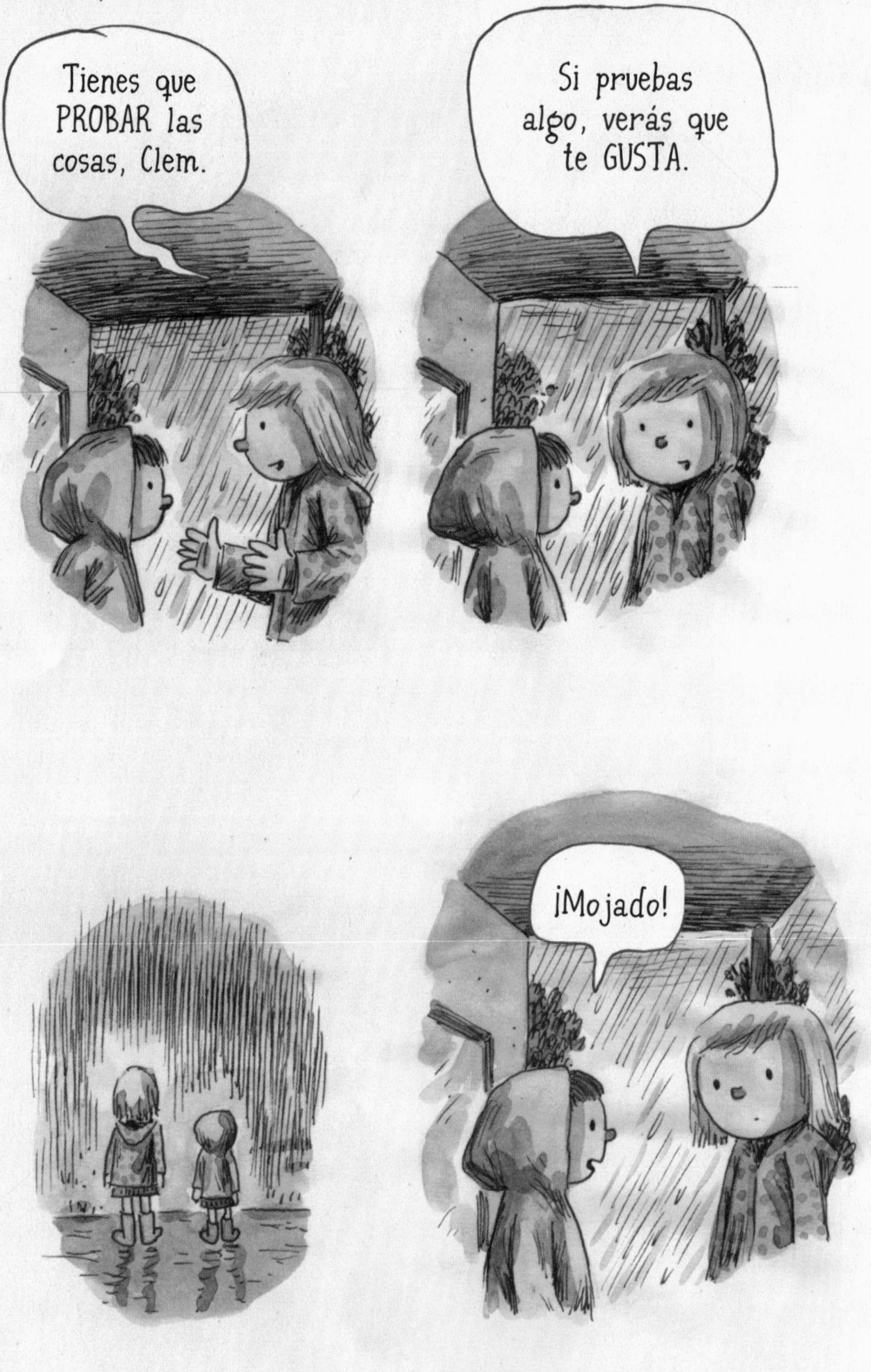
Tienes que PROBAR las cosas, Clem.
Si pruebas algo, verás que te GUSTA.
¡Mojado!

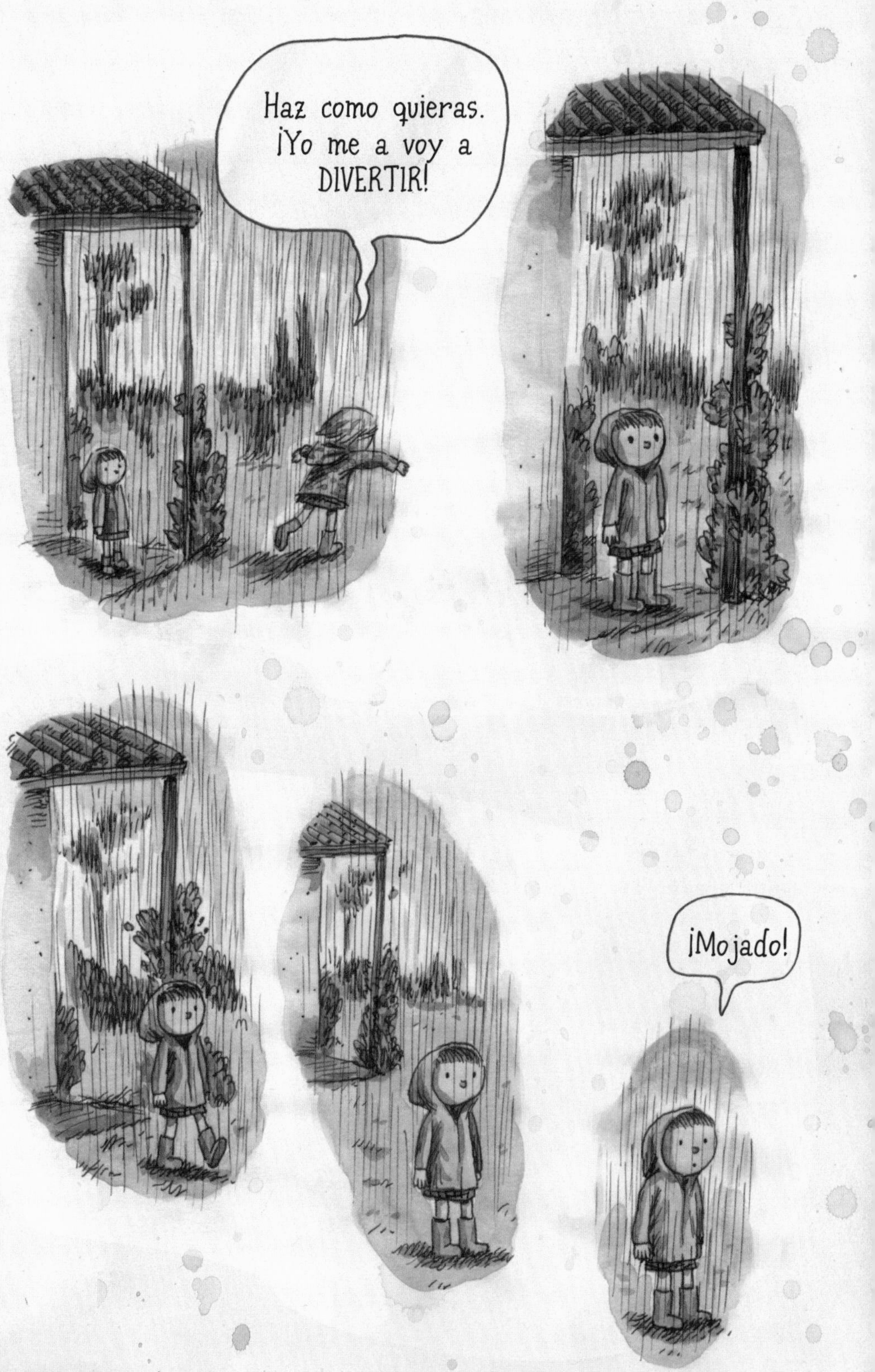
Haz como quieras. ¡Yo me a voy a DIVERTIR!
¡Mojado!

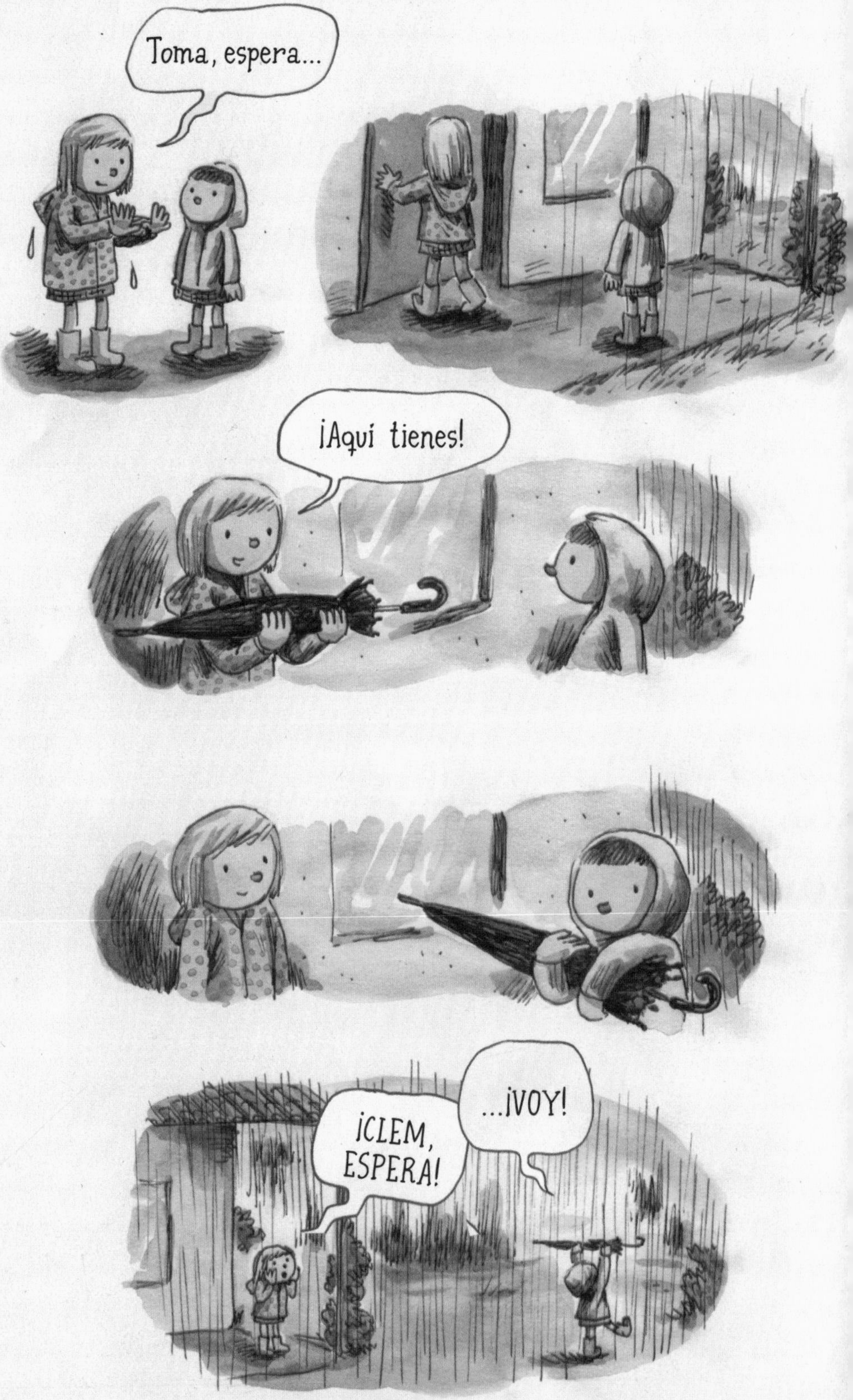
Toma, espera...
¡Aquí tienes!
¡CLEM, ESPERA!
...¡VOY!

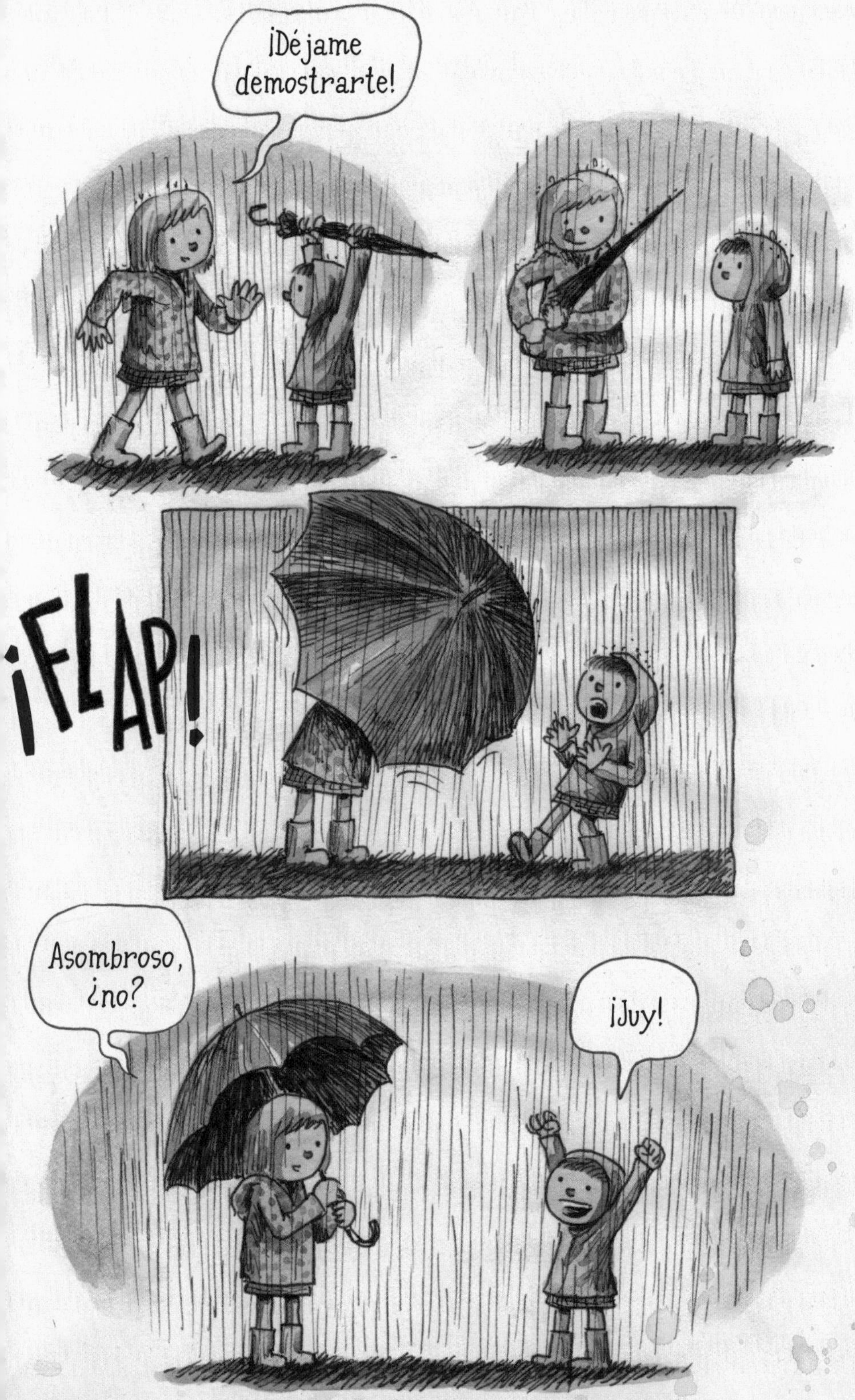
¡Déjame demostrarte!
¡FLAP!
Asombroso, ¿no?
¡Juy!

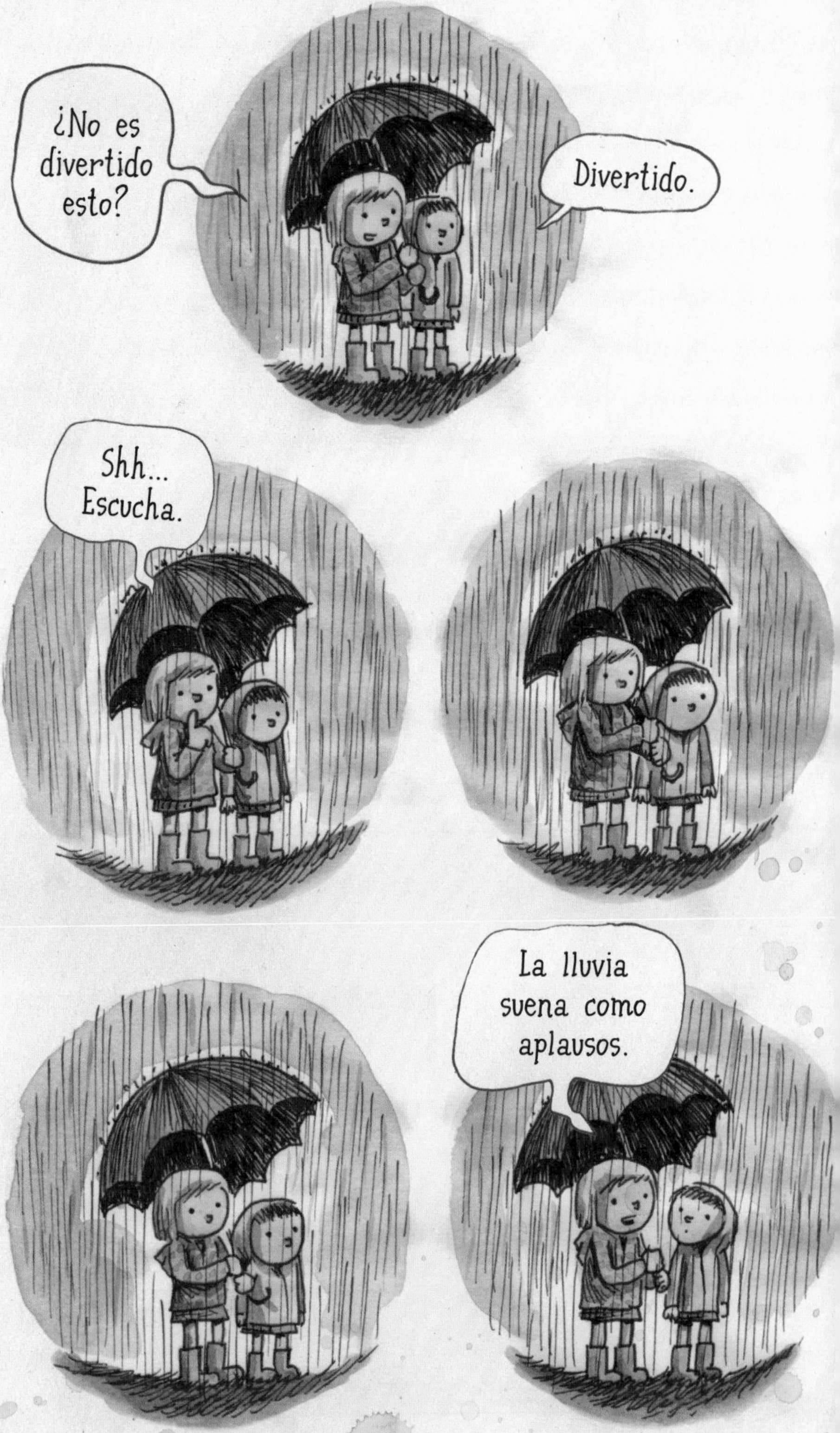
¿No es divertido esto?
Divertido.
Shh... Escucha.
La lluvia suena como aplausos.

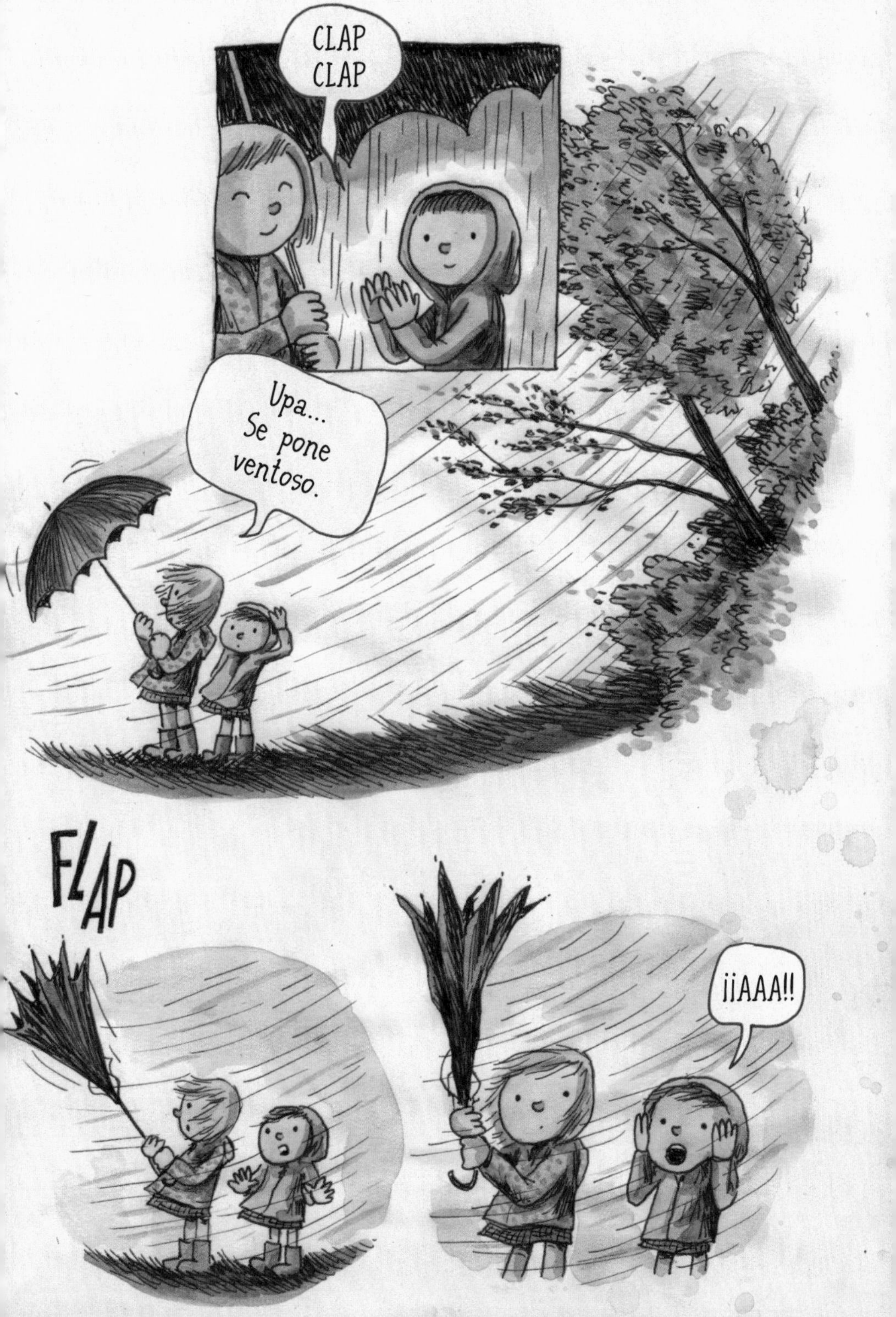
CLAP CLAP
Upa... Se pone ventoso.
FLAP
¡¡AAA!!

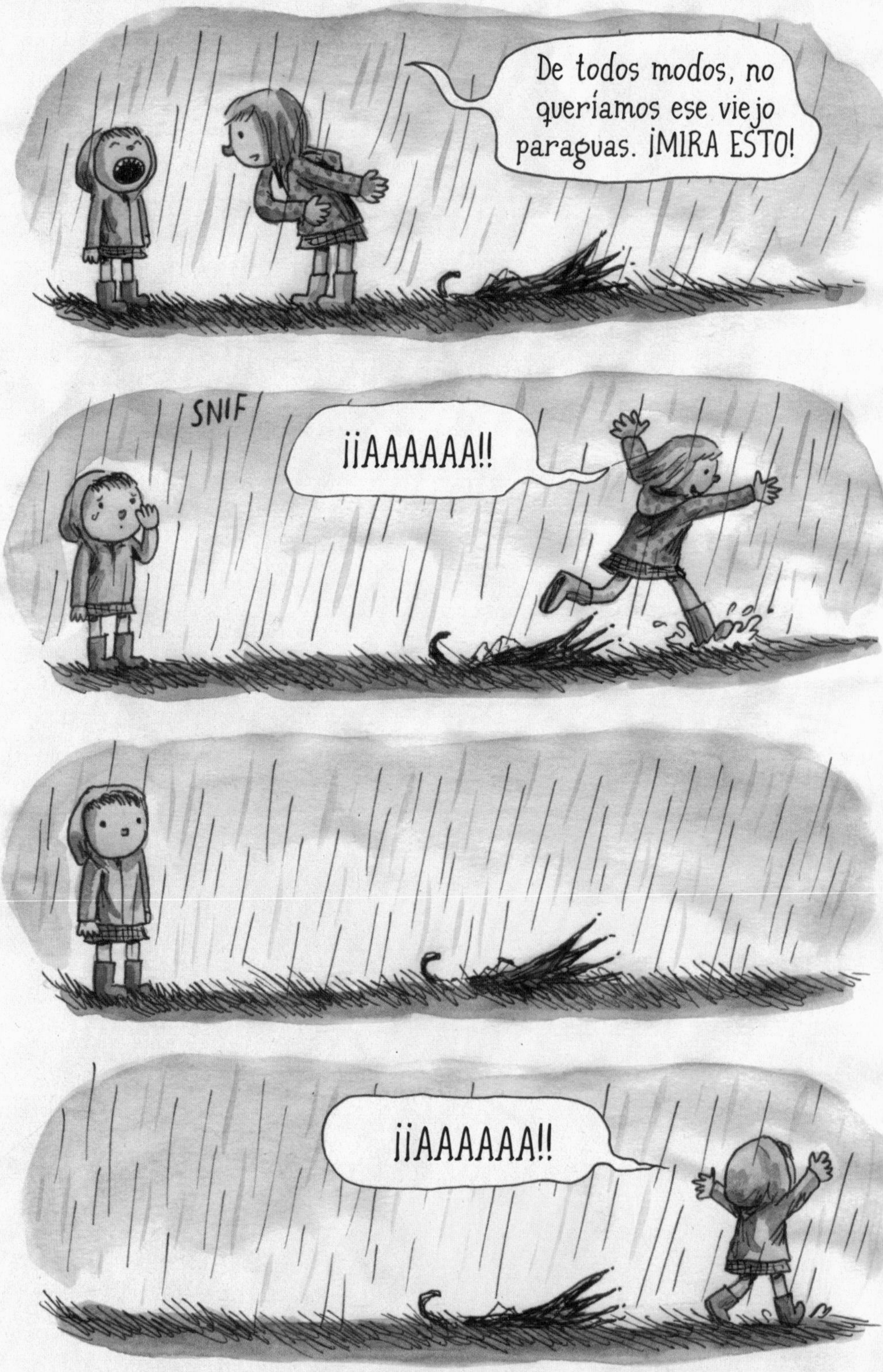
De todos modos, no queríamos ese viejo paraguas. ¡MIRA ESTO!
SNIF
¡¡AAAAAA!!
¡¡AAAAAA!!

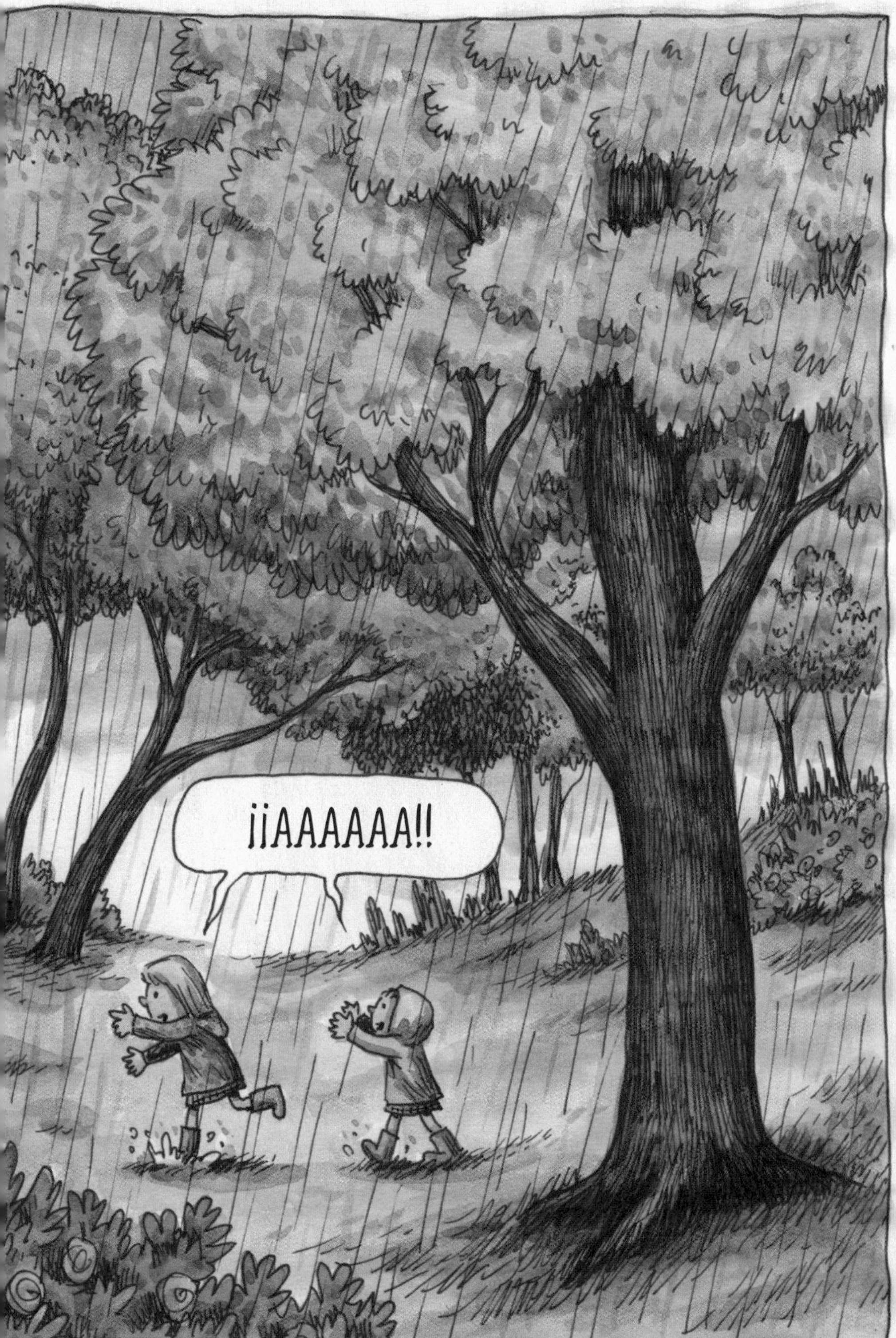
¡¡AAAAAA!!

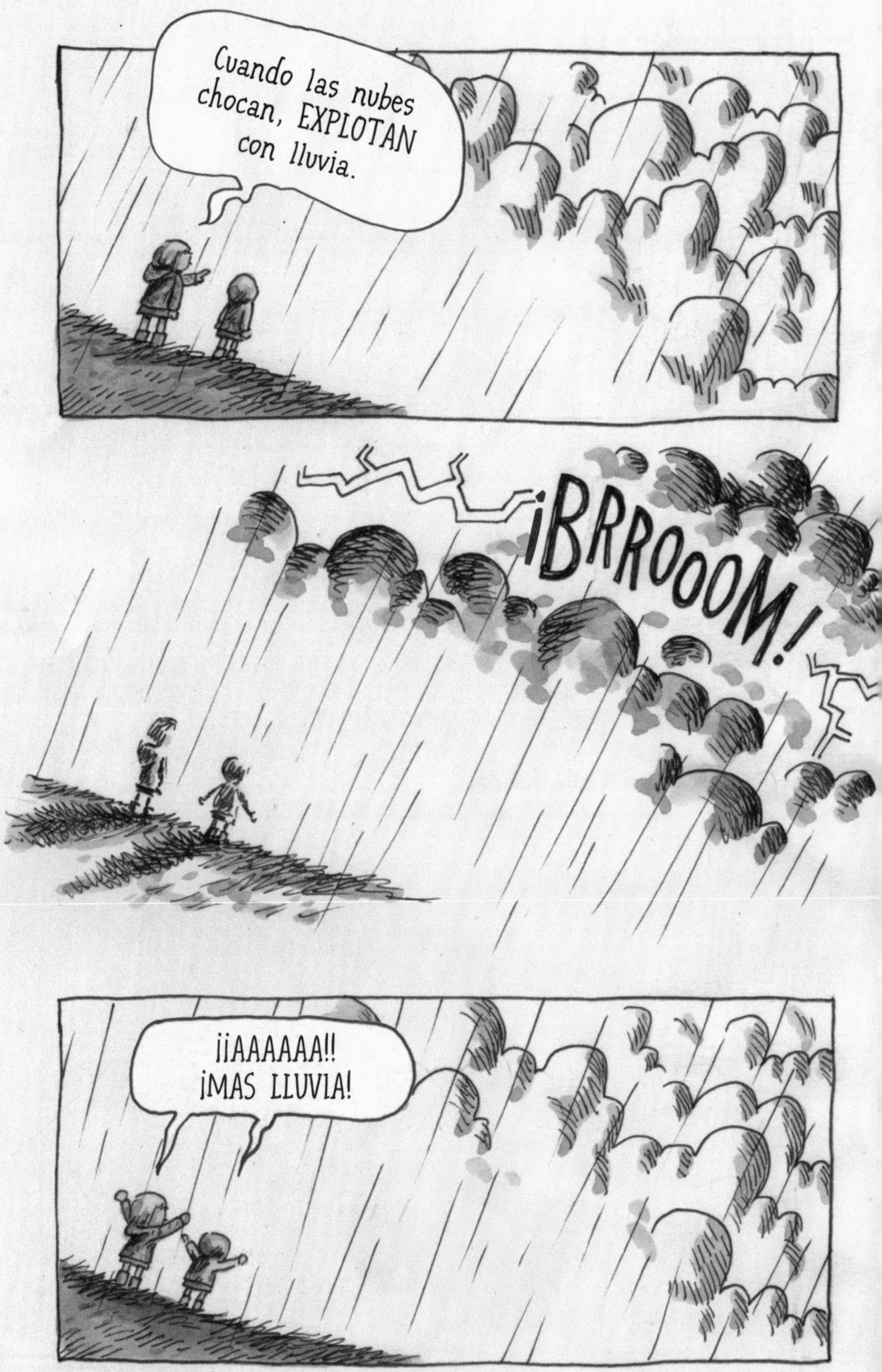
Cuando las nubes chocan, EXPLOTAN con lluvia.
¡BRRROOOM!
¡¡AAAAAA!!
¡MAS LLUVIA!

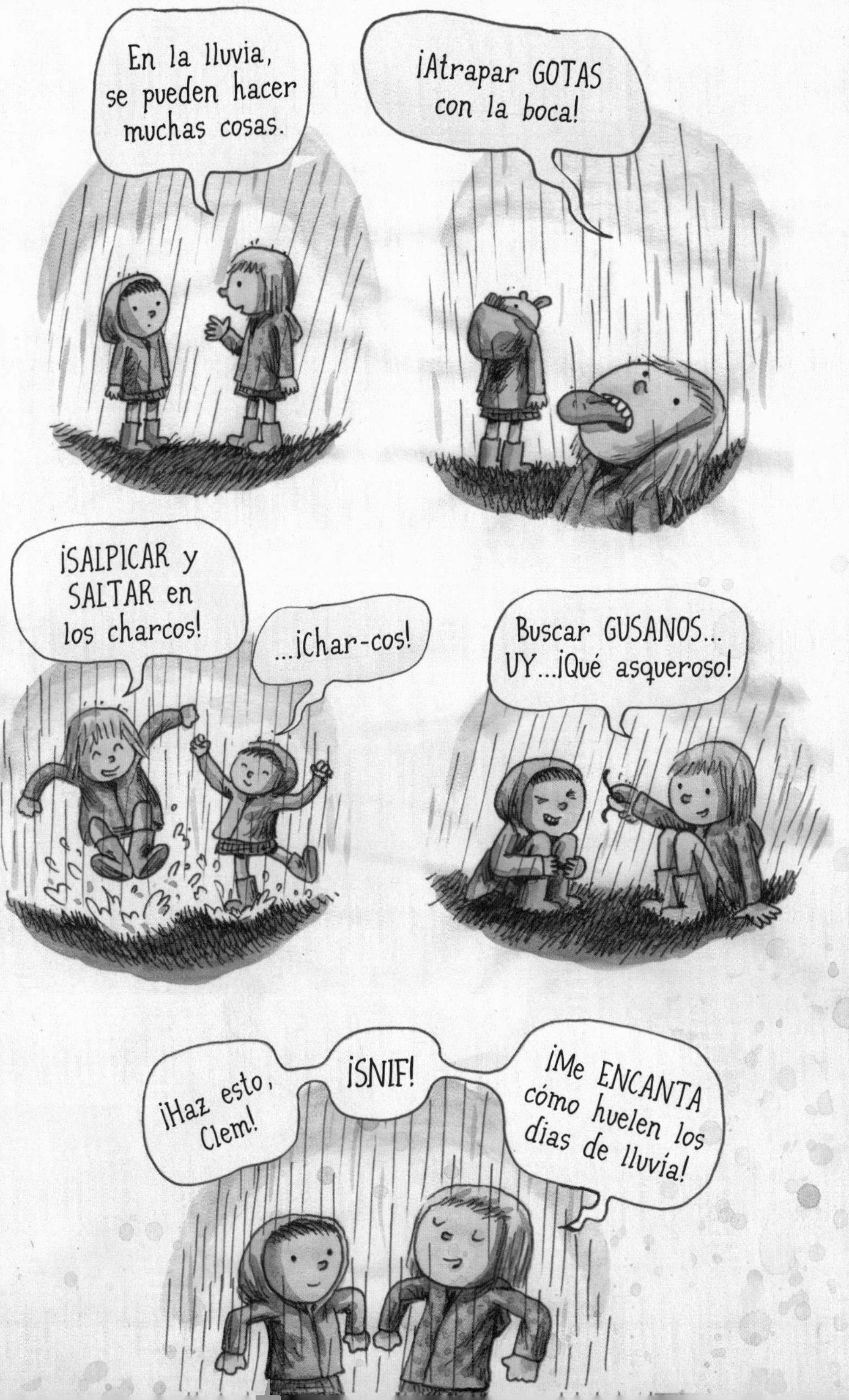
En la lluvia, se pueden hacer muchas cosas.
¡Atrapar GOTAS con la boca!
¡SALPICAR y SALTAR en los charcos!
...¡Char-cos!
Buscar GUSANOS... UY...¡Qué asqueroso!
¡Haz esto, Clem!
¡SNIF!
¡Me ENCANTA cómo huelen los días de lluvia!

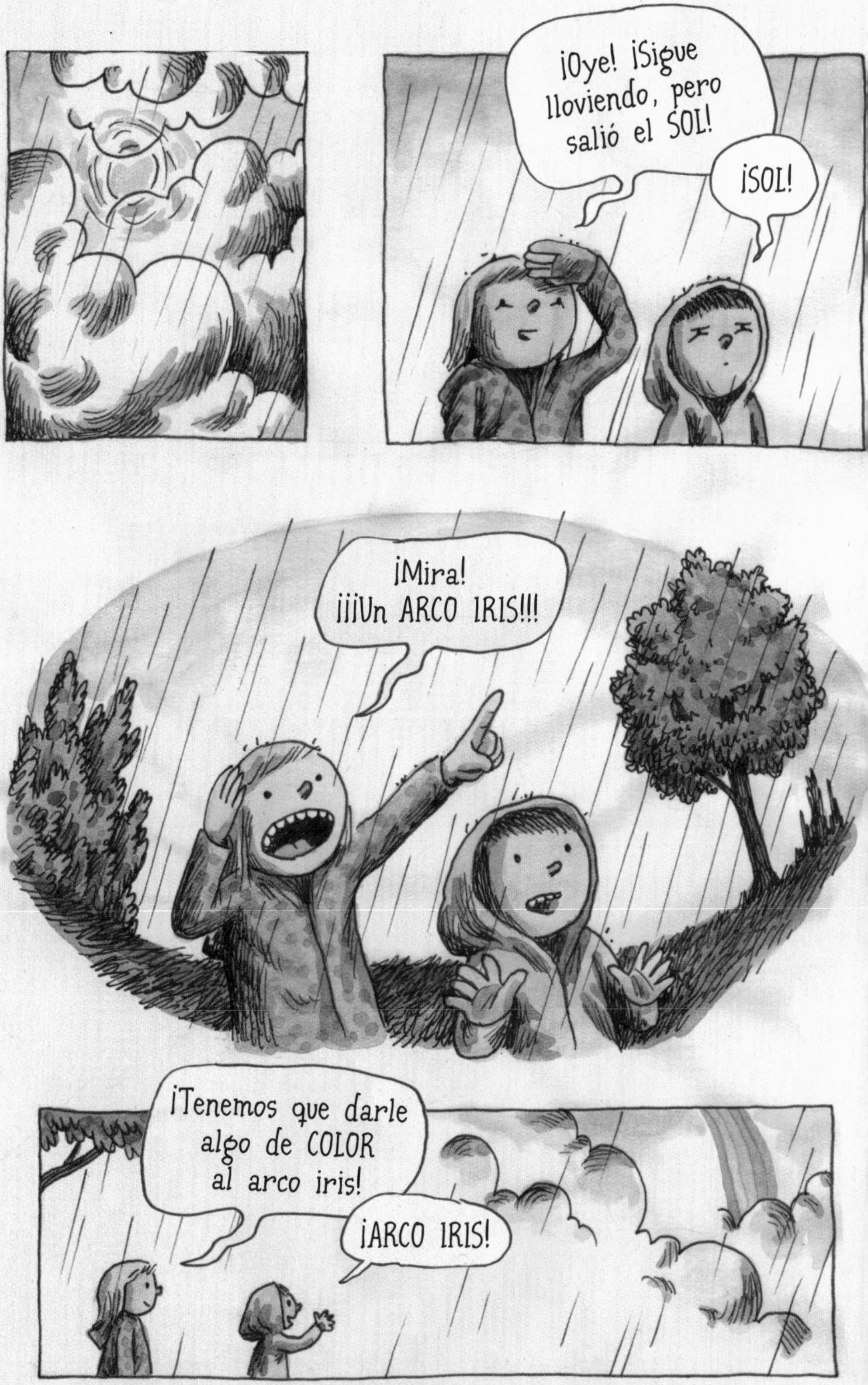
¡Oye! ¡Sigue lloviendo, pero salió el SOL!
¡SOL!
¡Mira! ¡¡¡Un ARCO IRIS!!!
¡Tenemos que darle algo de COLOR al arco iris!
¡ARCO IRIS!

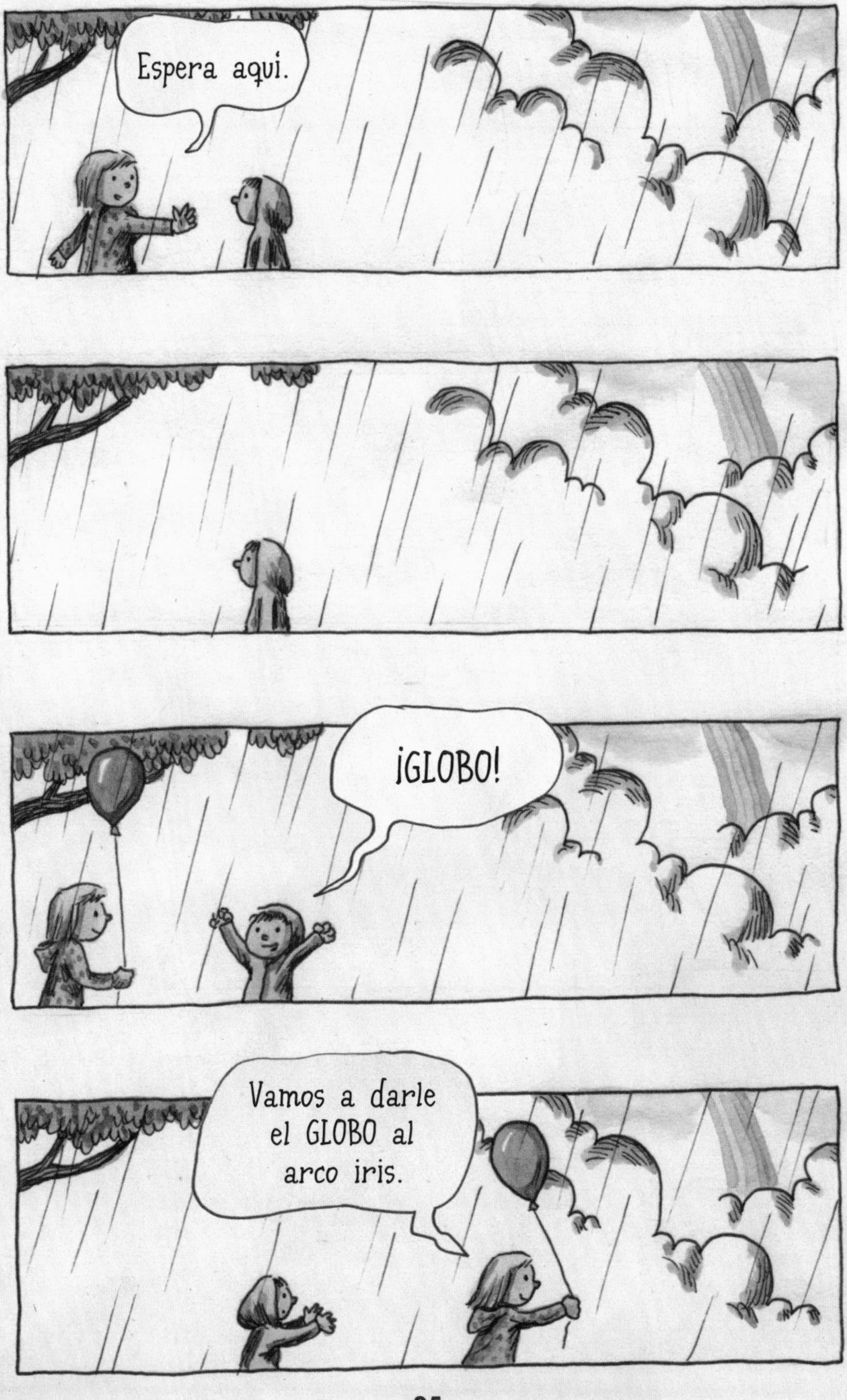
Espera aquí.
¡GLOBO!
Vamos a darle el GLOBO al arco iris.

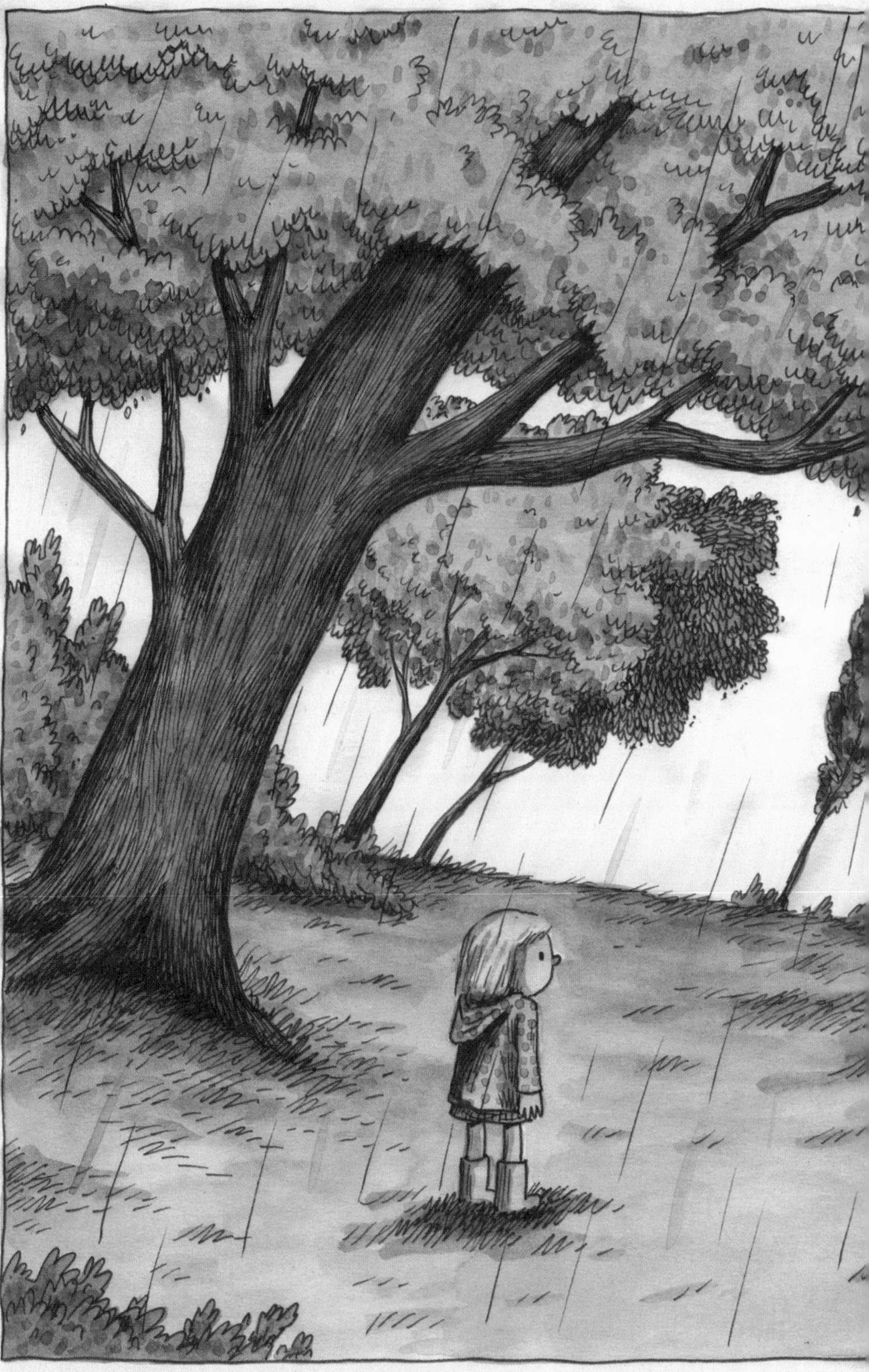

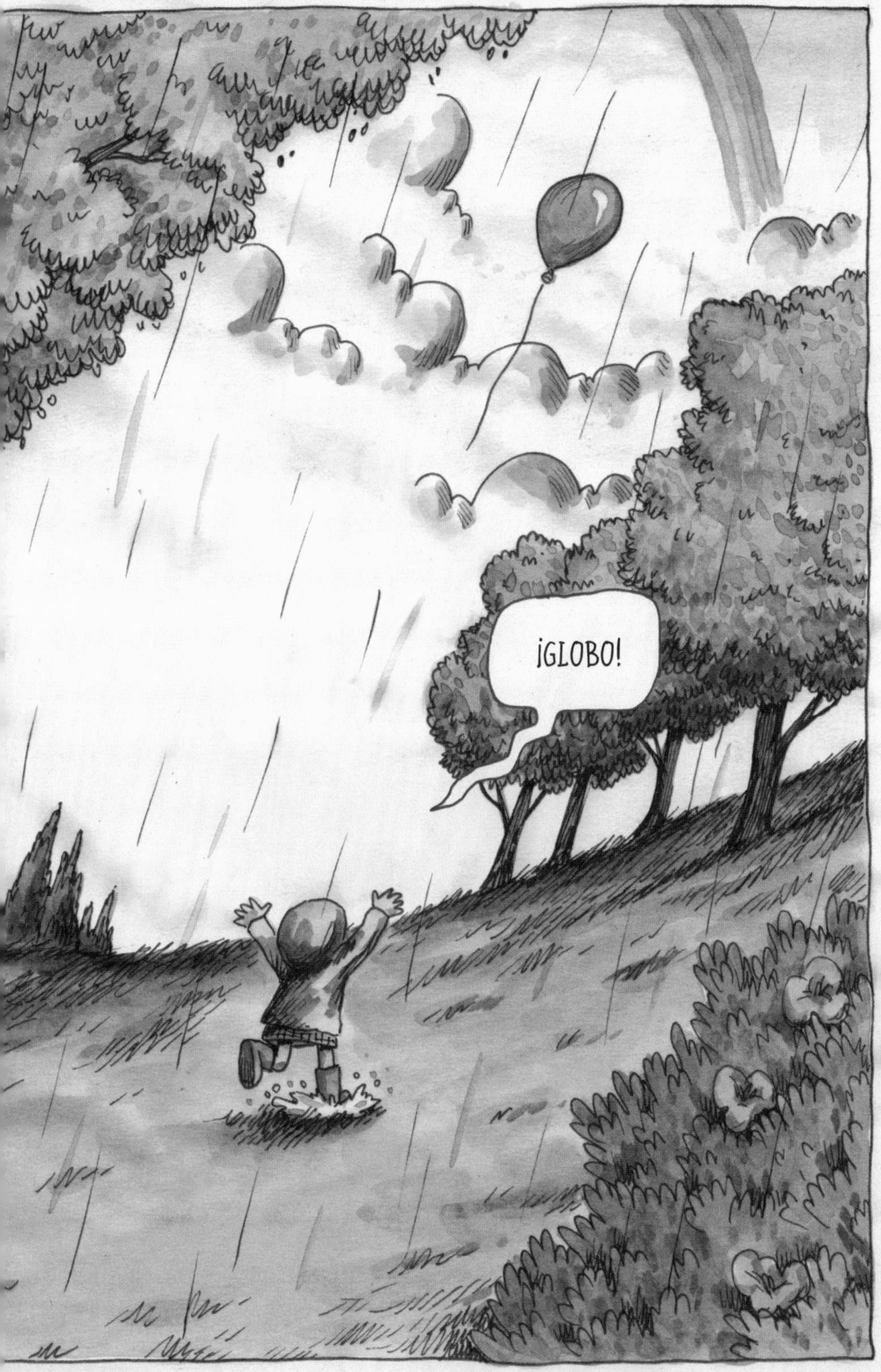
¡GLOBO!

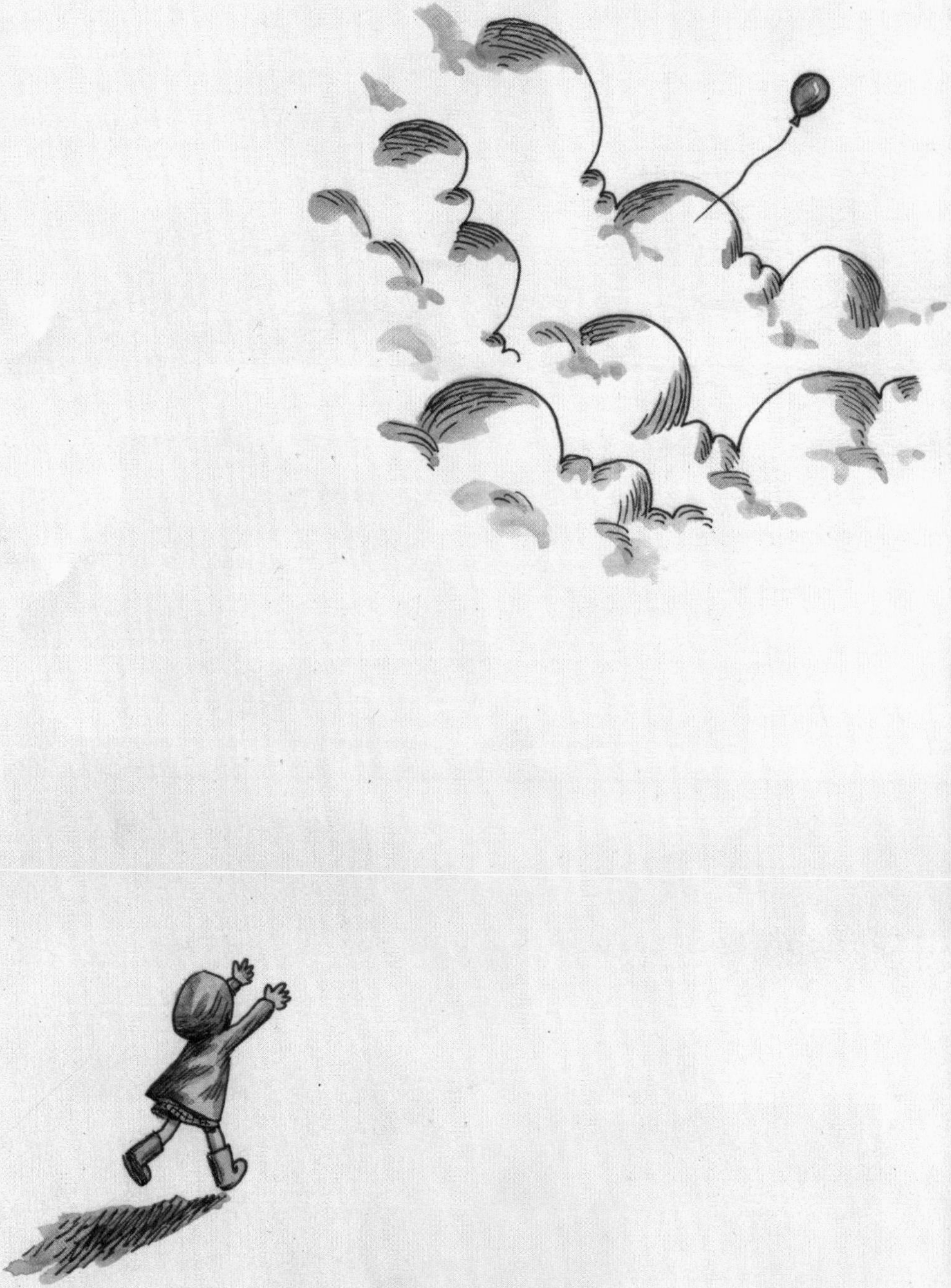

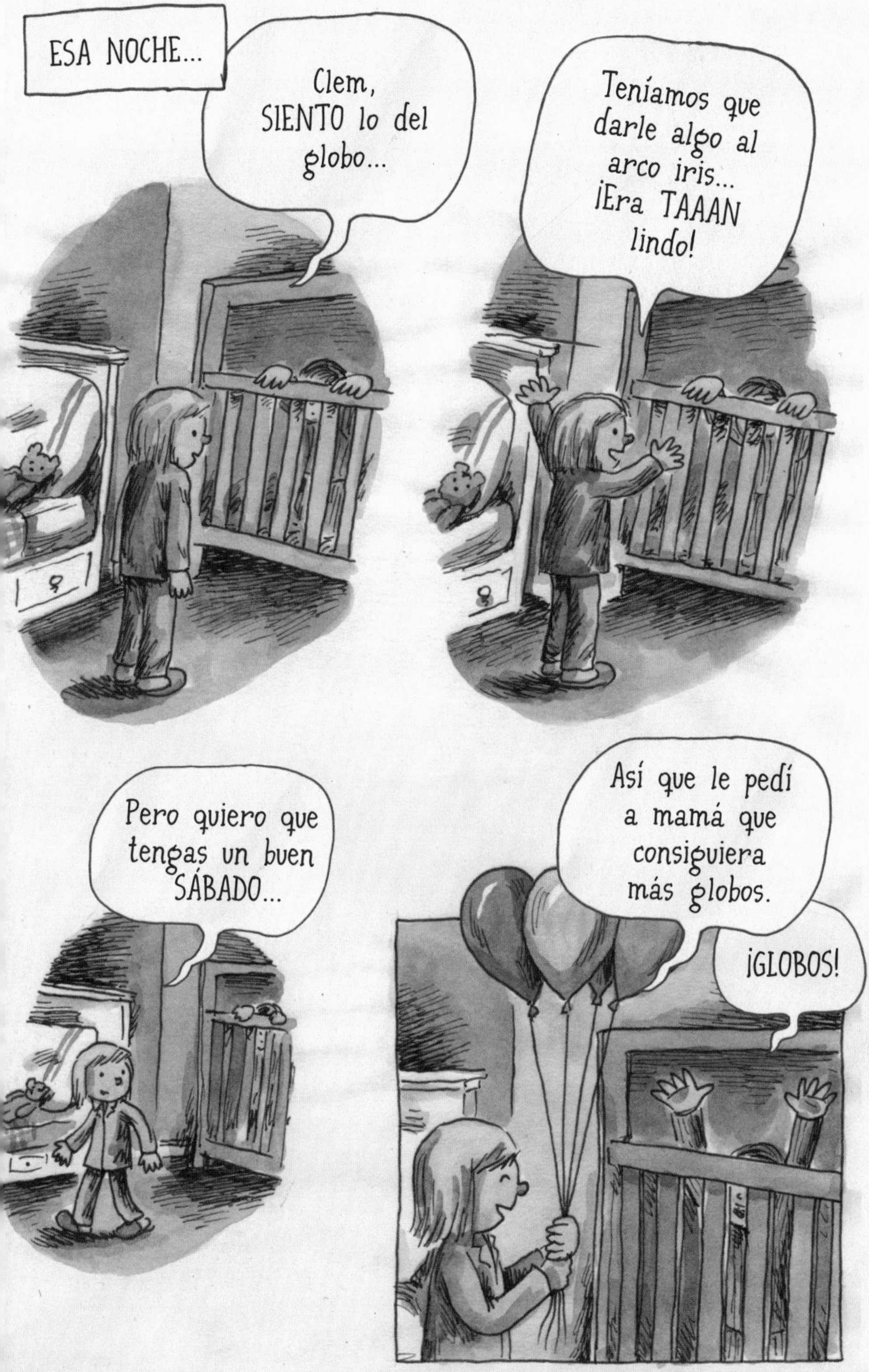
ESA NOCHE...
Clem, SIENTO lo del globo...
Teníamos que darle algo al arco iris... ¡Era TAAAN lindo!
Pero quiero que tengas un buen SÁBADO...
Así que le pedí a mamá que consiguiera más globos.
¡GLOBOS!

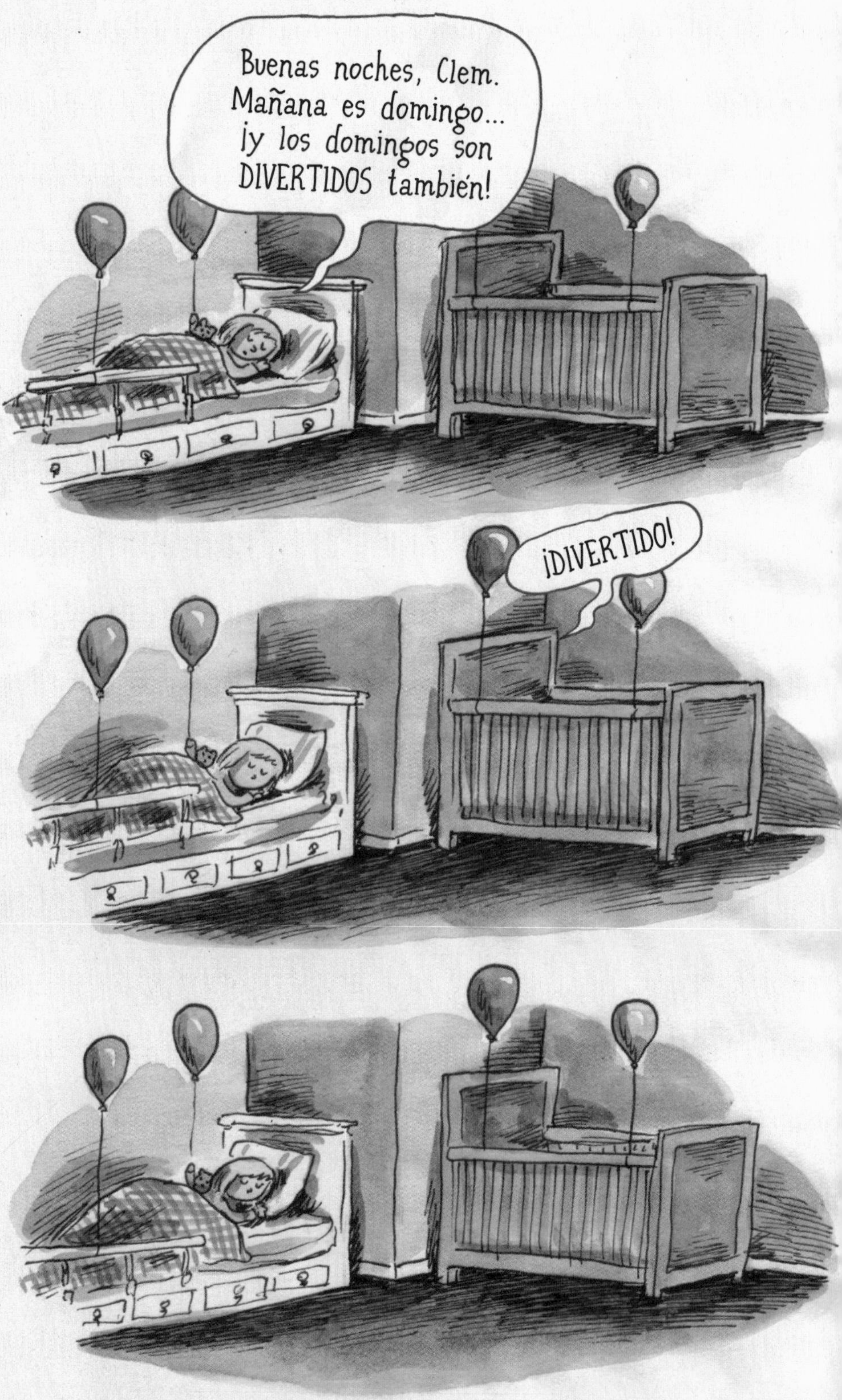
Buenas noches, Clem. Mañana es domingo... ¡y los domingos son DIVERTIDOS también!
¡DIVERTIDO!

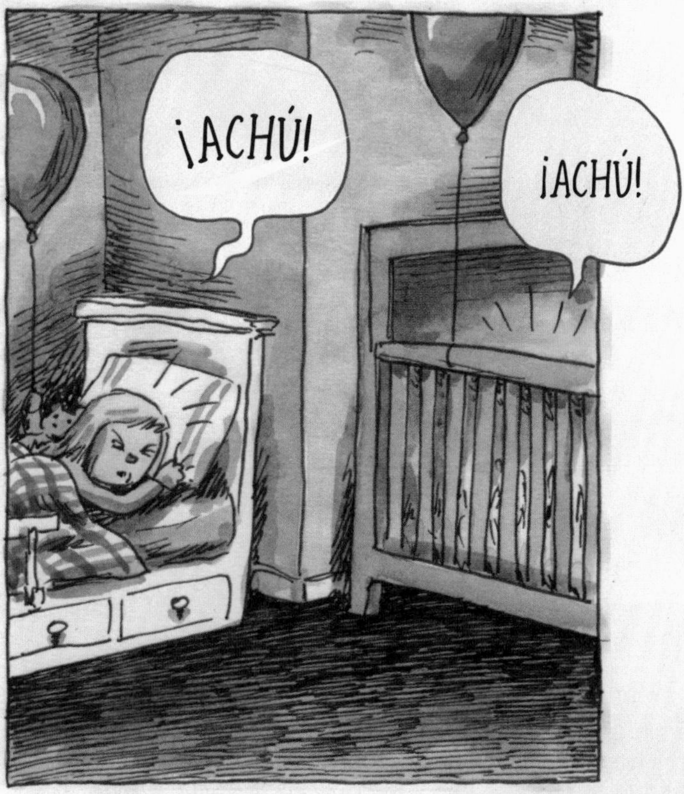
¡ACHÚ!
¡ACHÚ!

FIN

ABOUT THE AUTHOR
SOBRE EL AUTOR

RICARDO LINIERS SIRI lives in Buenos Aires with his wife and two daughters, Matilda, 5, and Clementina, 3, who inspired this story. For more than ten years, he has published a hugely popular daily strip, *Macanudo*, in the Argentine newspaper *La Nación*. He also tours the world drawing on stage with musician Kevin Johansen. His work has been published in nine countries from Brazil to the Czech Republic, but this is his first book in the United States. Like his daughters, Liniers likes rainy days even more than sunny ones.

RICARDO LINIERS SIRI vive en Buenos Aires con su esposa y sus dos hijas, Matilda (5) y Clementina (3), que fueron la inspiración para este cuento. Por mas de diez años publicó la tira diaria *Macanudo* en el periódico argentino, *La Nación*. El también viaja por el mundo haciendo dibujos en vivo con el músico Kevin Johansen. Sus libros se han publicado en nueve países, incluyendo Brasil y la República Checa, pero este es su primer libro en los Estados Unidos. Igual que a sus hijas, a Liniers la gustan más los días de lluvia que los días de sol.

—by Matilda, 5

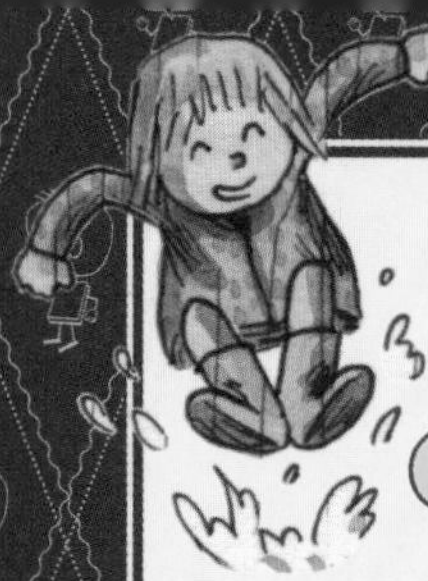

TIPS FOR PARENTS AND TEACHERS:

HOW TO READ COMICS WITH KIDS

Kids **love** comics! They are naturally drawn to the details in the pictures, which make them want to read the words. Comics beg for repeated readings and let both emerging and reluctant readers enjoy complex stories with a rich vocabulary. But since comics have their own grammar, here are a few tips for reading them with kids:

GUIDE YOUNG READERS: Use your finger to show your place in the text, but keep it at the bottom of the speaking character so it doesn't hide the very important facial expressions.

HAM IT UP! Think of the comic book story as a play and don't hesitate to read with expression and intonation. Assign parts or get kids to supply the sound effects, a great way to reinforce phonics skills.

LET THEM GUESS. Comics provide lots of context for the words, so emerging readers can make informed guesses. Like jigsaw puzzles, comics ask readers to make connections, so check a young audience's understanding by asking "What's this character thinking?" (but don't be surprised if a kid finds some of the comics' subtle details faster than you).

TALK ABOUT THE PICTURES. Point out how the artist paces the story with pauses (silent panels) or speeded-up action (a burst of short panels). Discuss how the size and shape of the panels carry meaning.

ABOVE ALL, ENJOY! There is of course never one right way to read, so go for the shared pleasure. Once children make the story happen in their imaginations, they have discovered the thrill of reading, and you won't be able to stop them. At that point, just go get them more books, and more comics.

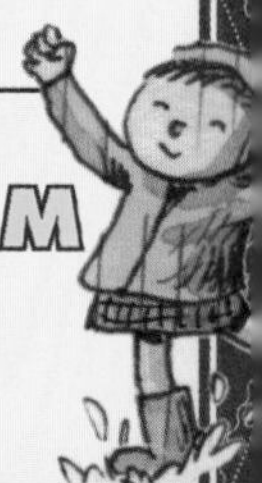